tiger tales
an imprint of ME Media, LLC
5 River Road, Suite 128, Wilton, CT 06897
Published in the United States 2012
Originally published in Great Britain 2012
by Hodder Children's Books
a division of Hachette Children's Books
Text copyright © 2012 David Conway
Illustrations copyright © 2012 Melanie Williamson
CIP data is available
ISBN-13: 978-1-58925-111-3
ISBN-10: 1-58925 -111-3
Printed in China
TLP0112

For more insight and
activities, visit us at
www.tigertalesbooks.com

THE GREAT FAIRY TALE DISASTER

by David Conway

Illustrated by Melanie Williamson

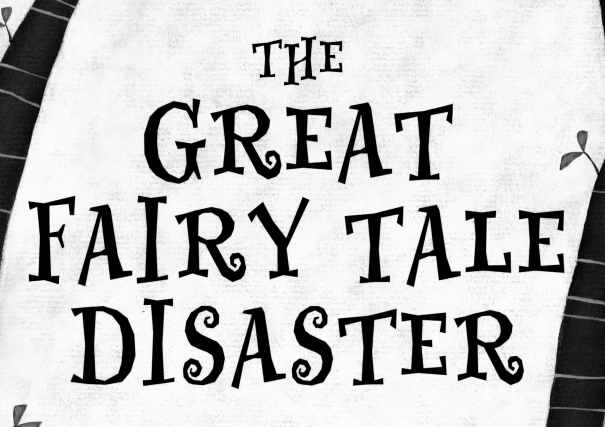

tiger tales

ONCE UPON A TIME, there lived an old Big Bad Wolf. He no longer had any huff and puff to blow down the **Three Little Pigs'** houses, and he'd had enough of falling into hot water.

"What I need," the wolf thought to himself, "is a nice **relaxing** fairy tale for a change." So he scampered off into the pages of the fairy tale book to find one.

Cinderella was busy sweeping and hadn't noticed the wolf's dark shadow appear in the doorway.

"I want to be in your tale!" he growled.
"Of c-oo-u-rr-se," stammered a frightened Cinderella.
"Take my place!"

Just then, the fairy godmother arrived.

"I know you'd love to go to the ball," she said to the wolf. "And so you shall!"

There was a flick of a wand and a burst of light. . . .

"Wolves don't wear dresses!"
cried the wolf, hobbling off in glass
slippers to find a different tale.

Soon after, the Big Bad Wolf crept up behind Jack on **the magic beanstalk.** Jack trembled as he let the wolf into his fairy tale.

The Big Bad Wolf was climbing up the bean-stalk when he saw two HUGE feet and heard a horrible giant voice bawling,

"FEE, FIE, FO, FUM!"

"This tale's too scary!" cried the wolf as he slid back down the beanstalk to find another one.

Then the Big Bad Wolf found Sleeping Beauty snoring softly in her bed. "WAKEY! WAKEY!" he snarled. "Out you go!"

There the Big Bad Wolf lay, so beautiful that the prince could not turn his eyes away. He knelt down and gave the wolf a kiss. . . .

"YUCK!" spluttered the Big Bad Wolf. "I'm not being kissed!" So he dashed away to try his luck elsewhere.

The Big Bad Wolf came to the Three Bears' empty cottage
in the forest. He opened the door and stepped into the tale.
"Yum!" he said. "Porridge! My favorite."

There the Big Bad Wolf lay, so beautiful that the prince could not turn his eyes away. He knelt down and gave the wolf a kiss. . . .

"YUCK!" spluttered the Big Bad Wolf. "I'm not being kissed!" So he dashed away to try his luck elsewhere.

The Big Bad Wolf came to the Three Bears' empty cottage in the forest. He opened the door and stepped into the tale. "Yum!" he said. "Porridge! My favorite."

The big bowl of porridge was too **hot**.

The second bowl was too **cold**.

But the littlest bowl was just right, so the wolf ate it **all up!**

"This is the life!" said the wolf as he sat down in the big, comfy chair. Suddenly the door opened and in stormed the Three Bears!

"Where's Goldilocks?" demanded Daddy Bear.

"What are you doing in our fairy tale?" scolded Mommy Bear.

"And where's my porridge?" cried Baby Bear.

The wolf made a run for it, but the **Three Bears** chased
after him into the next fairy tale. . . .

And then the next. . . .

And before you could say, "Mirror, mirror on the wall, who is the fairest of all?" there was chaos and confusion everywhere!

The **princess** didn't kiss a frog but she did kiss a **Billy Goat Gruff!**

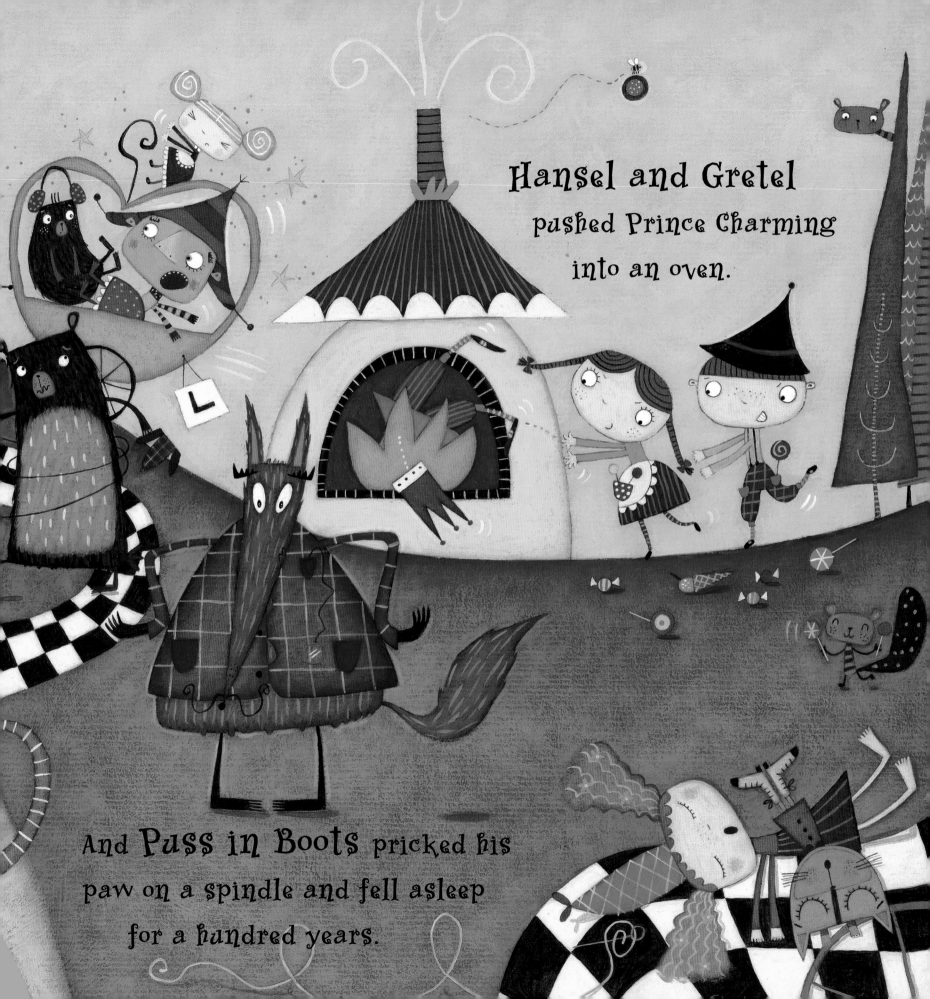

Hansel and Gretel pushed Prince Charming into an oven.

And Puss in Boots pricked his paw on a spindle and fell asleep for a hundred years.

"What a mess!" cried the Big Bad Wolf and he escaped back through the pages of the book to the Three Little Pigs.

"Little pigs! Little pigs! Let me come in!" huffed the Big Bad Wolf. "No, not by the hair of our chinny chin chins," said the little pigs. "We will NOT let you in."

But the wolf had already clambered up onto the roof and he was coming down the chimney . . .

only to land SPLASH in a pot of hot water!

"Oooh, not again!" cried the wolf.

And that was **the end** of the fairy tale troubles.